SUPER DC HEROES

SUPERMAN

TOYS OF TERROR

WRITTEN BY
CHRIS EVERHEART

ILLUSTRATED BY
JOHN DELANEY AND
LEE LOUGHRIDGE

SUPERMAN CREATED BY
JERRY SIEGEL AND
JOE SHUSTER

www.raintreepublishers.co.uk
Visit our website to find out
more information about
Raintree books.

Phone 0845 6044371
Fax +44 (0) 1865 312263
Email myorders@capstonepub.co.uk

Customers from outside the UK please telephone +44 1865 312262

Raintree is an imprint of Capstone Global Library Limited,
a company incorporated in England and Wales having its registered office at
7 Pilgrim Street, London, EC4V 6LB – Registered company number: 6695582

First published by Stone Arch Books in 2009
First published in hardback in the United Kingdom in 2010
Paperback edition first published in the United Kingdom in 2010
The moral rights of the proprietor have been asserted.

Art Director: Bob Lentz
Designer: Bob Lentz
UK Editor: Vaarunika Dharmapala
Originated by Capstone Global Library Ltd
Printed and bound in China by Leo Paper Products Ltd

ISBN 978 1 406214 86 4 (hardback)
14 13 12 11 10
10 9 8 7 6 5 4 3 2 1

ISBN 978 1 406215 00 7 (paperback)
14 13 12 11 10
10 9 8 7 6 5 4 3 2

British Library Cataloguing in Publication Data
A full catalogue record for this book is available from the British Library.

CONTENTS

CHAPTER 1

SURPRISE PACKAGES

The Christmas float pulled to a stop outside a toy shop in central Metropolis. A crowd of little kids cheered. Reporters Clark Kent and Lois Lane made their way through the smiling faces. They were here to write a story for their newspaper, the *Daily Planet*.

"This is the biggest crowd I've ever seen for the Christmas parade," said Lois.

"The ad on TV said there would be free toys," Clark said. "That always attracts a crowd."

The two reporters stopped near the float. A huge Christmas tree stood in the middle of the float. It sparkled with colourful twinkling lights. A pile of brightly wrapped presents sat under it.

The children cheered, looking for the jolly old man with a white beard. Instead a big, beefy man stepped on to the float. He wore a red Santa suit. His boots and belt were as black as his hair. He had mean eyes and a scar on his right cheek.

The crowd went silent. Some of the children frowned. A few of them turned away.

"Clark, isn't that –?" Lois began to ask.

Clark gave a quick nod. "Bruno 'Ugly' Mannheim," he said.

"Wasn't he in jail?" Lois asked.

"He was in jail," said Clark. "Superman caught him robbing a bank last year."

"Then what's he doing on that float?" asked Lois.

Clark watched Bruno closely. "Maybe he's here to steal Christmas," he joked.

Just then Bruno Mannheim spoke up. "Hello, children," he said. "I am so happy to see all of you! You see, I've just got out of jail. I learned a lot while paying for my crimes. I have been a bad, bad man. But starting today, I'm going to change." Bruno looked over at Clark and Lois.

"So that's his game," said Clark. "He wants us to think he's a good guy now."

Bruno raised his hands and continued, "Children of Metropolis, these are my gifts to you!"

Bruno reached under the tree and grabbed an armful of presents. He started throwing colourful boxes into the crowd. The children cheered.

"The kids certainly think he's a good guy now!" said Lois.

As the parade float neared the reporters, Bruno looked down at Lois. "Miss Lane, would you join me on the float?" he asked politely, holding out his hand. "You've been my toughest critic. I want to show you exactly how much I've changed."

Lois smiled and took a step toward the float. Clark Kent quickly grabbed her arm. "Be careful, Lois," he warned. "I have a funny feeling about this."

Lois smiled. "What's the matter?" she asked. "Jealous that I'm getting the scoop?"

Lois grabbed Bruno's hand and stepped on to the float. Wrapping paper was flying everywhere. The children shouted with joy as they saw their presents.

"You see, Miss Lane?" Bruno said, looking out at the crowd. "I've learned my lesson. I'm all about spreading joy and happiness."

Lois pointed towards the back of the float. A group of tough-looking men stood on the street, frowning. "If you're such a good guy, Bruno, why are those thugs still hanging around? They don't look joyful or happy to me," she said.

"Them?" said Bruno, smiling. "They're my bodyguards."

"You can fool children with a few gifts," said Lois. "But you can't fool me."

Bruno's mouth turned up in a crooked grin. "That hurts, Miss Lane," he said. Then he waved to some kids in the crowd. "Come up on the float, kids! Show everyone your presents."

Five kids jumped on the float. One boy waved his box. "It's a helicopter!" he shouted. "Cool!"

Bruno scowled. "A helicopter?" he asked, slightly puzzled.

A little girl held an open box over her head. "I got a helicopter, too!" she exclaimed.

All of the children opened boxes to discover the same toy.

"Those were supposed to be dolls and toy soldiers!" Bruno muttered. "What's going on?"

Suddenly, a girl screamed. Her little helicopter zoomed out of its box and flew around her head. Then all the other boxes burst apart. Every helicopter started flying.

The choppers circled the crowd. They buzzed just above the kids' heads. The tiny cannons on the toys squirted a sticky, yellow-orange liquid. The children screamed and started to run.

CHAPTER 2

RUNAWAY FLOAT

The little helicopters swarmed towards the float. Lois ducked the whirling blades.

"So this was your plan, Bruno?" she shouted. "This is bad even for you!"

Bruno waved off an attacking helicopter. "This wasn't supposed to happen!" he said. "I stole a load of dolls and toy soldiers from a warehouse! Someone switched them for these nasty choppers!"

Clark Kent called from the street, "Lois, look out!"

A group of helicopters circled in the air above the kids and their parents. Any second now, it looked like they were going to shoot more sticky liquid from their guns.

Near the float, Bruno's men were also dodging the helicopters. One crook pulled out a huge pistol and started shooting into the air, aiming to hit a helicopter.

BANG! He missed. The choppers attacked the thugs like a flock of angry metal birds. The men yelled and jumped into a nearby car for safety.

Clark looked around to make sure no one was watching him. Then he inhaled and blew out a huge super-breath. The circling helicopters went spinning away on the wind. Clark kept blowing until the dangerous toys were blown far down the street.

"The helicopters are flying away!" a kid yelled.

"Let's get out of here!" shouted another.

Then Clark heard tyres screeching. He looked over to see Bruno's Christmas float jump forward and speed away. Clark knew this was serious trouble. He started looking for a place to slip away and change into his Superman uniform.

The car carrying Bruno's thugs tore off after the float. They didn't want to let their boss get away without them.

On the float, Lois and the kids screamed. Bruno grabbed hold of the Christmas tree. He fell backwards, tearing off a branch. Presents flew off the float and scattered into the street.

"Who's driving the float?" yelled Lois.

"I don't know," Bruno answered.

Lois tried to gather the kids. "Lay down flat," she told them. "Hold on tight!"

Bruno was frightened. He shouted below to where the driver sat, "Stop this thing! Now!"

"You won't get away with kidnapping me and these children, Bruno!" shouted Lois.

"I'm not doing this!" Bruno cried.

The float raced down the street. It took a sharp turn around a corner.

SKREEE-EEE-EEECH!

Lois was thrown sideways and rolled across the deck of the float. To her surprise, she found herself staring into a small window in front of the driver.

Even though Lois was bundled up against the cold, a deep shiver went down her back. She realized now that Bruno Mannheim was telling the truth. The out-of-control float was not his idea. Lois could see into the driver's seat. She saw an evil smile, staring eyes, and a little bow tie. The crazy driver was not one of Bruno's men. It was Bruno's enemy.

The Toyman!

CHAPTER 3

THE TOYMAN

The Toyman always wore a mask with a horrible grin, but at this moment he sounded angry. "Move aside, Miss Lane!" he shouted. "I can't see where I'm going! Do you want me to have an accident?"

"Toyman!" shouted Lois. "I should have known!"

"But you didn't," the Toyman snapped. "My plan was perfect. And it's working."

"Attacking children with helicopters?" Lois said. "You should be ashamed!"

The float swerved as the Toyman jerked the wheel to the right. Lois held on tight.

"Bruno's the one who should be ashamed," the Toyman shouted. "He thinks he can clean up his image by giving away a few toys? Hah! I'll show him!"

Bruno crawled over to the window beside Lois Lane. His face was red with anger. "Toyman, you'll be sorry for this," he said.

The Toyman laughed. "You're the one who's going to be sorry," he said. "You'll wish that you'd never killed my father!"

"I didn't kill your father," Bruno said. "He killed himself!"

"Because you ruined his business!" shouted Toyman. "Now you'll finally pay!" He turned the steering wheel sharply. Bruno and Lois rolled away from the window.

The Toyman looked in his rearview mirror. He saw the black car filled with Bruno's men. They were close behind and catching up to the float.

"Here are some toys for your boys to play with," the Toyman sneered.

He pulled a lever next to the seat. A hatch opened under the float's rear bumper. Ten little windup robots dropped on to the street. They wandered around in circles, cranking and buzzing. When the black car reached them, the robots started exploding.

In the car, one of the thugs yelled, "Look out!" The driver swerved around the bursting robots. But the explosion rocked the car. The windows were blown out.

"Bruno must be crazy!" one of the men shouted. "Why is he trying to stop us?"

Toyman looked at the street ahead. There, standing in the middle of the road was a tall figure in red and blue. Superman!

"Drat his super-speed!" Toyman said to himself. "Those helicopters should have kept him busy longer."

Superman watched the float race towards him and the black car following behind. Using his X-ray vision, Superman searched the inside of the float. There, in the driver's seat, he recognized the Toyman. The children and Lois were in danger!

The Toyman pushed a button on the dashboard. "Good thing I planned for this," he said.

Superman saw a small door open on the front of the float. "What's he up to now?" Superman wondered.

A blast shot out of the little door like a machine gun. Superman saw a flock of yellow rubber duckies coming at him. They looked so cute and harmless. But Superman knew Toyman better. He wasn't surprised when the first ducky began to swell up like a giant balloon.

All of the duckies began to grow larger. Their rubbery sides stuck together. Soon, they had turned into a huge yellow barrier surrounding the Man of Steel. Then they puffed up even more. Superman was trapped inside a gigantic ball of rubber.

"Nice try, Toyman," said Superman.

The hero began to spin. The yellow ducky balloons span around with him. Faster and faster he whirled. The yellow rubber moved so quickly that it began to burn up. Soon, it had sizzled away. Bits of burning rubber duckies littered the street.

"Superman! Help!" cried Lois from the speeding float.

The kids' eyes were wide with fear. "Superman!" they screamed.

Superman decided he could catch up to the float in a minute. First he would take care of Bruno's thugs. He jumped back into the road. He set his feet down on the street and reached forward. The black car sped towards him. When the men inside saw the super hero, they all shouted at once. The tyres skidded and screeched, but it was too late.

The car slammed right into the Man of Steel. The front end folded up as if it hit a telephone pole. Superman skidded backwards as the car ground to a stop. The radiator smoked. The engine coughed and spluttered.

The thugs looked up at Superman, shocked and amazed.

"Sorry boys," Superman said. "I can't risk you running into someone while I'm trying to save your boss. I'll take care of Bruno and the Toyman."

"Toyman?" muttered one of the crooks. "Is he behind all this?"

Superman shot up into the air and out of sight.

CHAPTER 4

THE TOY FACTORY OF TERROR

The Toyman chuckled when he knew Superman was no longer in sight. He drove the float into a tunnel and descended below the city streets. The kids were scared in the dark. They huddled close to Lois.

"Where are we going?" Lois shouted.

"Yeah," said Bruno, "where do you think you're taking us?"

The Toyman didn't answer. Instead, he stopped the float in the middle of the tunnel. Steel doors opened in front of them.

Meanwhile, in the sky above Metropolis, Superman flew in search of the Toyman's float. He used his super-vision to magnify the streets below. He followed the route where Toyman and the float should have gone. But they were missing. Where could they be?

Underground, the float rolled through the steel doors. Inside was an old factory, piled high with broken toy parts. Dolls' heads and toy soldiers' arms were heaped on the floor. A thousand jack-in-the-boxes without the jacks leaned against the walls.

When the float finally stopped, Lois, Bruno, and the children got off. The strange scene scared the kids more than the dark tunnel. Some began to cry.

"Don't worry," said Lois. "Superman will find us. This will all be over soon."

The Toyman emerged from the float and looked down at his prisoners. His eyes were cruel and cold above his wide smile. "Yes. Don't worry, kids. Bruno will be finished soon," he told them.

"Let the kids go, Toyman," said Lois. "They didn't do anything to you."

"I don't care about them," the Toyman said. "I'm after Bruno. He owes me big-time. And nothing will stop me."

Bruno Mannheim stood up. "Take the kids, Toyman," he said. "You can ransom them back to their parents. You'll make a fortune. Just let me go."

Lois turned to the crook who was still dressed in his Santa outfit. "These are innocent kids," she said. Be a man and face the Toyman yourself!"

Bruno waved a hand. "Ah, Toyman won't hurt them. Especially since they're worth so much money."

CLINK CLINK CLINK

Lois turned to see the Toyman walking up a set of steel stairs. The mask with its weird grin was still stuck on his face.

"It's too bad these kids trusted Bruno," the Toyman said. "If they're foolish enough to trust this crook, they deserve what they get."

Soon the Toyman had reached a platform high above the factory floor. He pulled a remote control out of his pocket. "I've built a special toy for you, Bruno," he said. "I think your new young friends will enjoy it." Toyman pushed a button on the remote control.

Lois heard a bounce and a squeak. The noise grew louder. The kids pushed themselves closer. She hugged them tightly. **BOUNCE! SQUEAK!** A football bounced out from behind a pile of toy cars. It stopped in the middle of the floor.

Everyone relaxed. Lois sighed, and Bruno smiled.

"What's that supposed to be?" Bruno laughed. "You're going to kill me with a football?"

"It's so much more than a football," said the Toyman from his perch. He pushed another button on the remote. "Let's play," he said.

ZZRRRRTT! ZZRRRRTT! The football started to vibrate. Everyone closed their eyes, expecting it to blow up.

But instead of exploding, it opened with a **SNAP!** A dozen blades, sharp as razors, poked out of the ball. The ball started rolling across the floor. The squeak was gone. The sharp blades scraped as they moved against the concrete.

The children screamed.

The football rolled towards them. Lois grabbed the kids. She pulled them away from the deadly ball.

"Toyman, don't do this!" shouted Lois. She looked up at his perch. The little villain's evil mask glowed with happiness.

"I've finally got Bruno Mannheim right where I want him," the Toyman said. "I have him trapped, and Superman can't get in my way. It's brilliant. Don't you think, Miss Lane?"

Lois was scared. "Turn Bruno over to the police," she pleaded. "Let them take care of him."

"My super football is much more efficient, Miss Lane," Toyman said. He jumped back on to the floor and laughed. "And when it's done, there won't be anything left to find."

Lois looked over and saw Bruno climbing the Christmas tree on the float. "Get back here, you coward!" she shouted.

Bruno looked down at her and the kids. "Forget it. You're on your own," he called.

The football turned towards Lois and the children. It chased them into a corner. The knives were flashing and slicing through the air.

CHAPTER 5

TRAPPED!

"My life's work is almost done," the Toyman said. "I'll finally avenge my father's death."

"But these kids have fathers, too," said Lois, still huddling close to the children on the floor.

"Boo hoo," said the Toyman with a laugh.

"Hurry, children," shouted Lois. She pulled them back on to the float. "I think we'll be safe up here."

"Oh no!" shouted one of the kids.

A thin metal arm reached out of the football. It grabbed the side of the float and pulled itself up. The football started climbing on to the float. It was getting closer to the kids. They started to back away but couldn't go any further.

"Quick," said Lois. "Jump!"

The children jumped to the floor. Just then, the blades on the ball span like circular saws. They cut a path through the float like a soft stick of butter.

All eyes turned to the ceiling. A ray of sunlight poured through a hole. Then suddenly, the children saw a different ray of hope.

"Superman!" the children shouted.

In a second, Superman was on the float. He kicked the soccer ball away. The toy and its blades bounced against the factory wall.

"Blast you, Superman!" shouted the Toyman.

The Toyman pushed another button on his remote control. At his command, the football bounced off the wall and came flying back. This time it was spinning a hundred times faster than before.

"You won't ruin my revenge, Superman!" shouted the Toyman. "I'll cut you to super ribbons!"

Lois pointed and shouted, "Superman, look out!"

Superman turned and saw the football. It cut through the air at lightning speed. Superman span on one foot and threw a back kick. The ball bounced off his heel and flew towards the Toyman.

The little villain punched frantically at more buttons on his remote control. It was too late.

The bladed football spun upwards and then crashed down in front of him. Sparks flew off the metal. Then the ball flew past the Toyman, shredding his bow tie.

"Aaaahhhhhh!" Toyman screamed.

The ball smashed into the ceiling above his head and broke into pieces.

The Toyman ducked, trying to avoid the falling metal blades. His tiny shoe slipped on the floor. He fell backwards and landed in a pile of empty jack-in-the-boxes.

"No!" he cried.

Hundreds of boxes tumbled down, trapping the Toyman beneath their combined weight.

As the boxes moved, their handles turned. The factory was filled with the happy sounds of "Pop Goes the Weasel."

"I don't think this little weasel is going to pop up anytime soon," said Superman.

He turned to Lois and the children. "Don't worry, kids," he said. "You'll be back with your parents soon."

"Are you all right, Miss Lane?" Superman asked.

Just then, Bruno Mannheim climbed down from the top of the Christmas tree. "Whoa, that was close," he said. "What took you so long?"

Superman grinned. Then he looked at the dark factory. "The walls of Toyman's hideout are made of lead. I wasn't able to use my X-ray vision to find you.

"That slowed me down a little," Superman continued. "But then, thanks to Miss Lane's clues, I soon followed you here."

Bruno and the kids stared at her. "Her clues?" asked the crook.

"Yes," said Superman. "Miss Lane dropped her shoes along the road. Then she dropped her notepad. I followed the direction of the clues, and it led me straight to this abandoned building."

Lois looked down at her bare feet. Her shoes must have fallen off when the Toyman swerved the float back and forth along the road. In all the excitement, she hadn't even noticed they were gone.

"Quick thinking, Miss Lane," said Superman.

"Uh, thanks," she said.

Bruno held his hand out to the super hero. "Well, thanks loads, Superman," he said. "It's nice to be working together for a change. See you later."

"I've got someone coming to pick you up, Bruno," said Superman.

Bruno smiled. "My boys?" he asked, hopefully.

"No, *my* boys," Superman smiled.

A police siren sounded in the distance.

"Hey, wait a minute!" shouted Bruno. "The Toyman was after me. He was trying to kill me. I'm the victim here."

"And what about all those stolen presents you were going to hand out at the parade?" asked Superman.

Bruno frowned. "Oh, right." He looked at the broken dolls and soldiers that littered the Toyman's factory. The little villain had replaced them with his helicopters in the warehouse that Bruno had broken into earlier.

Lois stepped up to Superman. "I don't know how to thank you, Superman," she said. "You're always nearby when I –" She noticed the kids staring up at the Man of Steel. "I mean, when we need you."

"I wish I could stay, Miss Lane," he said, "but there's more crime to fight in Metropolis. The holidays are always a busy time."

"I can't wait to get back to the *Daily Planet* and write this story," said Lois. "Poor Clark is missing out on the whole thing."

Superman smiled. "Oh, I get the feeling Clark is nearby," he said.

The Man of Steel waved at the kids. He then grabbed Toyman and shot up through the hole in the roof. He became a red and blue streak, then disappeared.

"Well, kids," said Lois, staring up at the empty sky. "Merry Christmas."

WHO IS THE TOYMAN?

Winslow Schott Jr watched his father create wondrous toys for children. He hoped to one day follow in his father's footsteps. However, Winslow's dreams were shattered when his father was framed by gangster Bruno Mannheim and sent to prison. The experience twisted little Winslow's creative mind, transforming him into the Toyman. Armed with an arsenal of deadly toys, the Toyman pursues Bruno Mannheim, terrorizing all of Metropolis in the process.

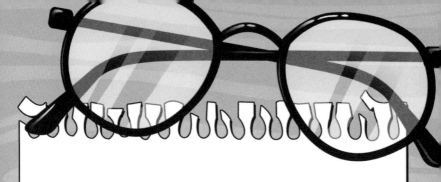

- Bruno Mannheim agreed to finance Schott Sr's toy factory, but used the facility as a front for his dirty dealings. When the Gotham Police descended upon the factory, Schott took the fall, leaving little Winslow to grow up in orphanages.

- Schott Jr has been known to toy with his foes. Once, Superman thought he had finally captured Schott, but the real Toyman flipped a switch and detonated a radio-controlled double!

- The Toyman isn't concerned with the safety of children. He often devises schemes that take advantage of them. In an attempt to frame the Man of Steel, the Toyman once designed Superman dolls that turned on their owners.

- Unable to relate to others, Schott once created a living doll to give himself a friend. Named Darci Mason, the living doll resembled a real human in every way. Later, Darci left the Toyman to become a famous fashion model.

BIOGRAPHIES

Chris Everheart always dreamed of interesting places, fascinating people, and exciting adventures. He is still a dreamer. He enjoys writing thrilling stories about young heroes who live in a world that doesn't always understand them. Chris plans to travel to every continent on the globe, see interesting places, meet fascinating people, and have exciting adventures.

John Delaney is an award-winning storyboard artist, director, animator and design artist with over 20 years of experience in both live-action production and animation. For the past 15 years John has also worked as a comic book artist for DC Comics and Bongo Comics. He has pencilled a wide variety of characters such as Superman, Batman, Wonder Woman, and the Justice League, as well as shows like *Dexter's Laboratory*, *Scooby-Doo*, *Futurama*, *The Simpsons*, and many more.

Lee Loughridge has been working in comics for more than 14 years. He currently lives in a tent on the beach.

GLOSSARY

avenge pay someone back for wrongdoings

coward someone who is easily scared and runs away from scary situations

descended went downward

inhaled breathed in

frantically did something wildly with excitement or fear

lever bar that you use to control a machine

ransom money that is demanded before a prisoner will be set free

scattered moved hurriedly in different directions

scoop story reported in a newspaper before others have a chance to report it

villain wicked or evil person

DISCUSSION QUESTIONS

1. Bruno tries to give children toys to make everybody like him. Do you think his desire to change from bad to good was real? Why or why not?

2. Superman gives Lois credit for something she did on accident. Have you ever been thanked, or punished, for something you didn't mean to do? Explain.

3. Do you think Superman should keep his true identity secret? What would be the positives and negatives of telling everyone that he is Clark Kent?

WRITING PROMPTS

1. Superman's secret identity is Clark Kent, mild-mannered reporter. If you had a secret identity, what would it be? How would living two lives be challenging?

2. The Toyman has created lots of weird toys. Create a plan for your own toy. What does it look like? What does it do? After you explain how it works, draw a picture of your new toy.

3. The people of Metropolis hold a parade as a celebration of the holidays. What celebrations do you participate in? Which celebration was your favourite? Why?